Weekly Reader Children's Book Club presents

BEAR MOUSE

BEAR MOUSE

by Berniece Freschet

Illustrated by Donald Carrick

Charles Scribner's Sons / New York

Printed in the United States of America

Library of Congress Catalog Card Number 72-13745

SBN 684-13320-2

Weekly Reader Children's Book Club Edition

For Dinah Sue, with special love

The snow was deep.

A thick quilt of white covered the meadow, drifting high against a stone wall.

Branches on the pine and birch bent low.

Under the soft quilt, a meadow mouse, shaggy as a little bear, ran down a snow tunnel.

Her path crossed another, and she quickly turned, following along the new mouse-trail.

There were many of these snowy tunnels rambling through the meadow—a network of pathways that crossed and crossed again—worn smooth by the constant drumming of tiny mouse-feet.

Suddenly the little mouse stopped.

She sat up on her hind legs.

She sat very still.

Every muscle in her small body was tense. She had many enemies to look out for! What had she heard?

A gray squirrel....

Or the soft, padded paws of a weasel overhead?

The red fox slinking near?

Or did she sense that the weasel and the bobcat were out on the prowl for a meal of mouse, watching for the slightest telltale movement in the snow.

Her small ears, almost hidden under her coarse fur, listened for the slightest sound. She flicked an ear, brushing it against the tunnel wall.

She heard the musical tinkling of snow-crystals falling. Then all was quiet.

Soon she hurried on, down the pathway.

Another meadow mouse ran toward her. For a moment they stopped, their noses twitching...touching. They squeezed past each other, and then off they scrambled in opposite directions, each intent on getting to somewhere.

A moment later the mouse pushed into an opening and down to her nest among a tangle of twisted roots.

It was a good place, cozy and warm.

In the middle of the nest, snuggled together on a soft bed of dry grasses, lay four tiny mouse-babies.

They smelled their mother's nearness and squeaked their hunger. The tiny mice wanted their dinner. But there was little milk for the week-old babies.

During her last hunt, the meadow mouse had found only one dried hazelnut to eat. This was not enough nourishment to make the milk to feed her hungry young.

Gently the mother mouse pushed her nose into the soft mound of fur, her pink tongue licking each tiny mouse-baby.

She chirruped soft sounds of comfort.

But the mouse knew she could not stay long....She must find something more to eat.

In nervous, jerky movements, she circled her babies. Then with one last quick turn, she left the nest, hurrying off down a snow tunnel. She moved into a trail that led upward and soon popped her head out of the snow.

She looked around, black, shiny eyes watching for signs of danger. All seemed safe. The little mouse came out of her tunnel and scurried to the foot of a gnarled old pine tree.

Sunlight sparkled on the white snow. There was a sudden flash of red as a cardinal flew out of the tree and swooped away across the meadow.

The mouse sat up, and with her front paws, she carefully cleaned the snow from her coat of fur. She looked different from most other kinds of mice.

Instead of a narrow pointed head, her head was round.

Instead of a sleek, smooth body, hers was chunky.

She had small ears and a hairy tail. Her legs were short, and her long, dark-brown hair made her legs seem even shorter. Because of her shaggy coat of fur, she looked like a "bear mouse."

The little meadow mouse was very hungry.

In the summer, when food was plentiful, she liked to eat seeds, roots, and berries, and her favorite food of sweet clover, and tender plants of alfalfa.

But now the snow was deep and food was hard to find. Winter had come early this year, and the mouse's storehouse of seeds was already gone.

She poked her nose into a crack in the tree, looking for a bite of something—a weed seed, or maybe a dry tuft of moss. But she found nothing. She often visited the old pine tree and had long ago picked it clean of every seed, every nut, every dry blade of grass.

High above in the blue sky, a hawk glided over the meadow. He swooped down, the black shadow of his wings skimming across the white snow.

Silently, nearer he glided.

The meadow mouse sat very still.

She sensed danger.

The hawk dipped low. Sharp talons opened wide.

With a squeak, the mouse dived into the snow and scurried down a tunnel. Soon she stopped and crouched against the snow-path to rest.

She listened. Except for the wild beating of her heart, all was still.

When her fear passed, she hurried on. She came to a path that led up to the pond. Maybe she would find something to eat there. Up she scrambled.

Turtle Pond was frozen over....Winter's quiet had come to the pond. The songbirds were gone, and many creatures were in hibernation, sleeping away the long, cold months.

The duck family who made their home here in the summer had flown to a warmer land. And the playful otters had long ago left for the big river.

The old bullfrog, the water snake, and the turtles were asleep, burrowed deep in the mud at the bottom of the pond.

Only the bigmouth bass and a few water creatures still swam under their roof of ice.

At the edge of the pond the mouse hunted for a snail, or a water bug that might be caught in the snow. But the sparrows had already found and snapped up the trapped insects, and there were no snails here, only two dry shells.

The mouse's stomach felt very empty. She licked at the snow.

She darted under an alder bush and looked for a stray leaf or two that might still be clinging there. But the bush was bare, stripped clean by the deer. There was something else though....

A cocoon hanging from a stem. *Food!*

Quickly the mouse ran up the stem. Holding the cocoon in her front paws, she ate it all. When she was finished, she ran under the low-hanging branches of a small spruce tree, and here she sat, daintily cleaning her whiskers.

She felt better now, but she was still hungry.

Soon out she dashed, scurrying for the stone wall at the side of the meadow, leaving behind her a lacy trail of footprints in the soft snow.

The sun was low in the sky, and the mouse would have to return to her babies soon, but first she needed more to eat. She had to find food to make milk for her young, or they would starve.

Overhead the cardinal flashed by. Something dropped from his bill. A red holly berry lay in the snow.

The mouse hurried toward it. It was dangerous for her to be out in the open, but hunger made the mouse forget caution. She picked up the berry and began to nibble it.

High in the gnarled old pine tree, a snowy owl looked out across the still, white meadow. He spread his great wings and sailed upward.

"Whooo—whoo—whoo—" he called softly.

The little mouse heard the hunting cry of the owl and she darted for the safety of the stone wall. She crouched, waiting, her small body trembling with fear and hunger.

A snowshoe rabbit huddled near—one long ear bending forward. Quickly, in zigzagging leaps he bounded away, hurrying for safe cover among the blackberry bushes.

For a while the mouse stayed close to the stone wall. But a sense of urgency began to trouble her....She had been away from her nest for too long. Even though she had not found food, she must return to her babies. The little mouse started across the meadow.

Suddenly she stopped. A strange, wild scent filled the air.

The little mouse stood high. She looked around, turning her head to one side and then to the other, her ears twisting this way and that, listening for the slightest sound.

She sniffed the air.

At the edge of the meadow, a bobcat slunk low.
He crept forward, toward the mouse.

Slowly, nearer and nearer crept the bobcat.

Now he was close enough—

He pounced!

The mouse leaped to one side.

Again the bobcat sprang!

The mouse dodged to the other side—

Twisting and turning, the little mouse raced for the safety of the stone wall—the cat at her heels.

She was almost to the wall.

With a great bound, the bobcat leaped forward—

The mouse felt sharp claws rake her fur.

End over end, she somersaulted across the snow.

In a last, desperate leap, the mouse sprang for the wall, squeezing herself into a crack between the stones.

The cat pushed a paw inside, his sharp claws stretching toward the mouse, but he could not reach her. The little mouse was safe.

With an angry snarl the bobcat turned and trotted away to look for his supper at the pond.

Her narrow escape and her hunger had exhausted the mouse. Her strength was almost gone. She was too weak now to return to her nest and her young.

She lay huddled against a rock, her small sides heaving.

She rested.

She nibbled a dry tuft of grass wedged between the stones. It was not much but it helped to fill the hollow place in her empty stomach. With her forepaws she pulled at the grass.

Suddenly, out of the crack between the stones, spilled a cache of acorns and weed seeds—a squirrel's forgotten storehouse of food.

Today the little mouse was lucky.

She ate and ate until her small stomach could not hold one single seed more. Then she stuffed her cheeks full, and away she raced—back to her tunnels in the snow— back to her nest and her family.

With tiny squeaks of delight, the mouse-babies welcomed their mother. She pulled them close.

When their stomachs were stretched tight with the warm milk, the mouse-babies snuggled into their mother's shaggy fur. Safe and warm in their cozy nest, the mouse-family went to sleep.